Visit us at SequoiaKidsBooks.com for bonus downloadable content.

Consultant: Manuel Román-Lacayo

Photography © Shutterstock 2024
Sergio Hayashi; AS Foodstudio; Jose Luis Samayoa; fizkes; Brent Hofacker, Byron Ortiz

Published by Sequoia Children's Publishing,
an imprint of Sequoia Publishing & Media, LLC

Sequoia Publishing & Media, LLC,
a division of Phoenix International Publications, Inc.

8501 West Higgins Road, Chicago, Illinois 60631
34 Seymour Street, London W1H 7JE
Heimhuder Straße 81, 20148 Hamburg

© 2024 Sequoia Publishing & Media, LLC

CustomerService@PhoenixInternational.com

Sequoia Children's Publishing and associated logo are registered trademarks of Sequoia Publishing & Media, LLC.

All rights reserved. This publication may not be reproduced in whole or in part by any means without permission from the copyright owners. Permission is never granted for commercial purposes.

This book is sold subject to the condition that it shall not, by way of trade or otherwise, be lent, resold, hired out, or otherwise circulated without the publisher's prior consent in any form or binding or cover other than that in which it is published and without similar condition being imposed on the subsequent purchaser.

www.PhoenixInternational.com

ISBN: 978-1-64269-432-1

Quincy Goes to the Latin American Festival

Written by Mari Bolte
Illustrated by Amber Gayle

Taste the WORLD!
Created by Alyx Douglas

sequoia children's publishing

An imprint of PHOENIX International Publications, Inc.

Hello and *hola!* My name is Quincy. Are you ready to go on an adventure?

Today, we are going to a Latin American festival. My town holds one every year. It is a time to celebrate the food, culture, and history of Central America and Mexico. There are musicians and dancers. People sell arts and crafts inspired by their homelands. There is even a big parade!

But I am most excited to try new flavors. There are dozens of people making food. They have samples of traditional dishes to taste. Trying things that are different from what I eat every day is so much fun! I'm going to ask the vendors for recipes. Then, I can make them later with my family!

I learned in school that Mexico is the northernmost country in Latin America. Central America is the land between Mexico and South America. Most of the vendors here today are from Mexico or Central America.

Mexico and Central America are some of the most diverse places in the world! There are 826 different Indigenous groups spread across Latin America. Those are people who are native to the area.

People crossed the land to trade or hunt. They looked for new homes. Colonizers from Spain settled there later. They brought a common language. Enslaved people from Africa brought their own culture and recipes with them. Food is a way for people to express themselves. It is a hands-on way to experience culture and history. And it's the tastiest way to learn something new!

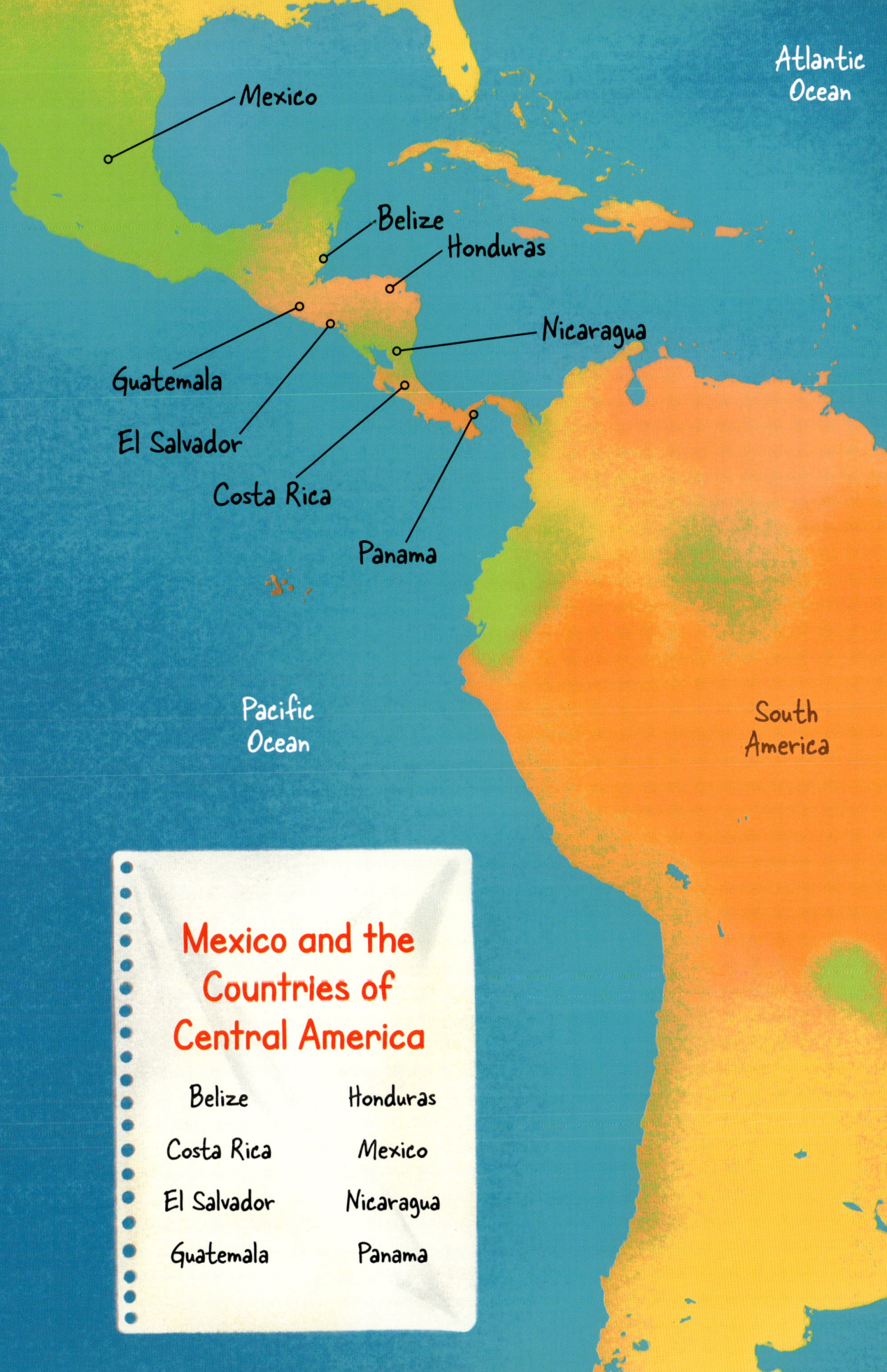

Oh, look, tortillas! Many people in Latin America eat tortillas. They are made from flour or corn. I wonder what kind they are making?

"Today, I am making corn tortillas," the vendor says. I watch as they roll a ball of tortilla dough, which is called masa. It is set on a metal plate. Then, another plate goes on top. They press down on a lever. The top plate is removed. Now, there is a perfect and flat tortilla!

"What is that?" I ask, pointing.

"This is a tortilla press," the vendor says. "This one belonged to my mama.

Food Fact: Corn flour comes in many colors. Yellow is common, but white and blue are also sold worldwide. The flavors are slightly different. Yellow tastes the most like corn. White has a more delicate flavor and makes softer tortillas. Blue flour is sweeter and nuttier.

"When I was a child in Mexico, we ate tortillas every day. We would go to *Abuela's* house after school to help her make them. You can use tortillas for everything. My mother stuffed them with meat or vegetables to make tacos. We used them to scoop up beans or salsa. When you fry them, they are crispy and delicious.

"First, you make the dough. The main ingredient is called *masa harina*. It's a flour made from corn. Abuela used to make hers from fresh corn, but today you can buy it at the store. You mix it with water. Abuela had a special bowl and spoon she only used for making tortillas. My brother's favorite job was to stir everything together. The dough gets very thick. It is hard work!

"Can you smell it?" continued the vendor. "It's almost like standing in the middle of Abuela's garden in the summer.

"Everyone helped roll tortillas in my family. You help with tortillas, or you don't get to eat any!

"If you have a tortilla press, you can use that to make the dough flat. But Abuela liked to do everything the way her mother showed her. She had a heavy cast-iron skillet. It was my job to push down on the skillet.

"I always dreamed of making one huge tortilla, wrapping myself in it like a blanket, and taking a *siesta*!"

Recipe: Corn Tortillas

Ingredients:

- 1 cup instant corn masa (masa harina)
- ¾ cup water
- ¼ teaspoon salt

Steps:

1. Pour the masa, water, and salt into a bowl. Mix until all the water is absorbed. This will take 2 to 3 minutes. If the dough looks too dry, add a little more water.

2. Let the dough rest for 15 to 20 minutes. While the dough rests, ask an adult to preheat a griddle or skillet over medium-high heat.

3. Divide the tortilla dough into about 10 balls. Cover with a damp towel or place in a plastic bag to keep the dough from drying out.

4. Place a ball between two pieces of plastic wrap or waxed paper. Use a heavy skillet or a rolling pin to flatten the dough.

5. Place a tortilla on the skillet. Cook for 20 to 30 seconds. Carefully flip the tortilla over. Cook for 20 to 30 more seconds. Repeat. The tortilla should bubble or puff. Repeat a final time. Then, place the warm tortilla under a clean kitchen towel.

Tip: Uncooked dough balls can be stored in an unsealed plastic bag. Refrigerate them for up to 3 days. Cooked tortillas can be stored in a sealed plastic bag for 10 days.

That was so much fun! When you listen to people's stories, it's almost like you're there with them. And I have tortillas to eat now and a recipe to try later. I'm going to look for masa harina at the grocery store. The tortilla vendor said I can find it in the baking aisle. There are so many ways to eat tortillas. Maybe I'll learn more ways to enjoy them from these other food vendors.

The people at this booth are Nicaraguan. Something smells delicious! "What is this?" I ask.

"It is called *gallo pinto*," the cook says. "Gallo pinto means 'spotted rooster' in Spanish." The dark beans in the white rice do look like a rooster's feathers!

"Rice and beans is a popular dish in Latin America," he tells me. "In Nicaragua, gallo pinto can be served at every meal.

Food Fact: Enslaved people brought recipes for rice and peas with them from Africa. When they arrived in the Americas, they realized beans made a good substitute.

"Gallo pinto is the perfect way to use up old rice," the vendor explains. "Day-old rice is best. My papá always made extra the night before. I also have a secret method when I'm short on time. Leftover rice from my favorite take-out place works just as well! Shh. Don't tell Papá!

"Nicaraguan gallo pinto uses special small red beans, but any dried beans will do. They need to be soaked overnight. Then, they are boiled. We mix the bean broth with the rice.

"To make the gallo pinto, the rice and beans are fried together. The rice and beans are no longer separate ingredients. They make the perfect pairing. My father would put cheese and crema on top to make it extra delicious."

I can't wait to make this at home. It's going to make the best breakfast ever. I want an egg on top and a little hot sauce. I'll have all the energy I need to get through the day!

Recipe: Gallo Pinto

Ingredients:

- 1 cup dried red beans
- ⅓ cup uncooked white rice (or 1 cup day-old cooked rice)
- 1 teaspoon salt
- 1 tablespoon vegetable oil
- ⅓ cup diced onion
- 1 garlic clove, minced
- Crema or sour cream
- Queso fresco

Steps:

1. The night before, cover the beans completely with water. Set them out of the way.

2. Next, make the rice. Combine one part rice to two parts water in a pot. With an adult's help, cook over medium heat until the water boils. Place a lid on the pot and reduce the heat to low. Simmer for 15 minutes or until all the water is absorbed. Take the pot off the heat and let sit for 10 minutes. Then, use a fork to fluff the rice. Pour the rice into a bowl and refrigerate overnight.

3. Drain the beans in a colander the next day. Pour the beans into a pot. Cover with clean water and sprinkle in salt. Boil for 20 minutes or until the beans are soft. Use a ladle to spoon around a cup of bean liquid into a bowl. Set the bowl aside. Then, have an adult drain the cooked beans.

4. Ask the adult to heat the oil in a large pan over medium-high heat. Add the onion and garlic. Stir until the onions have softened. Add the beans and a little bean liquid. Stir until the beans start to pop a little. Then, add the rice. Add bean liquid as needed to give the rice more color. Cook for 5 to 10 minutes or until the rice is as dark as you like. Top with crema and queso fresco.

Tip: Using day-old rice and dried beans keeps the textures from being mushy.

I think it is time for dessert. What's this? I wonder what this Guatemalan chef is making.

"Today, I will show you all how to make champurradas," the chef says to the crowd. She pauses. "What are we making?"

"Cham-pooooor-AH-duhs," the crowd says together.

"That's right!" the chef says, smiling. "They are the perfect sweet treat. In Guatemala, we eat champurradas with coffee, hot chocolate, or atol, a warm drink made with corn.

"In Guatemala, it is easy to find champurradas at markets or bakeries. Champurradas are Guatemalan, but they share roots with Spanish and Italian cookies. Masa harina is the main ingredient. Corn can be used for everything!

"The cookies are sweetened with a special sugar called *piloncillo*. It's a type of raw sugar that is sold in the shape of a cone. We grate it when we need to use it. You can get a similar flavor from brown sugar. It's not quite the same, but it's still delicious.

"Sesame seeds are sprinkled on top of each cookie. It makes them look pretty and also gives them a faint nutty taste. The Spanish brought us sesame seeds, but we were quick to add them to our own recipes.

Food Fact: There are between 21 and 23 Indigenous Mayan populations in Guatemala, as well as other non-Mayan Indigenous people. They lived there for more than 3,000 years before Spanish colonizers arrived in 1518. The mixture of Spanish and Mayan flavors influenced the country's food and people.

"Now that you know how to make your own champurradas, what will you do next?" the chef asks.

"Make them at home!" the audience calls back.

"I expect to be invited to all your homes for hot chocolate!" the chef says, grinning.

Masa harina is used in so many ways! We can have masa for breakfast, lunch, and dinner. For 9,000 years, corn fed people across Central America and Mexico. And it's still feeding us today.

Recipe: Champurradas

Ingredients:

- 1 stick butter, softened
- ½ cup brown sugar
- 2 tablespoons molasses
- 1 cup flour
- ½ cup masa harina
- 1 teaspoon baking powder
- Pinch of salt
- 1 teaspoon vanilla
- Sesame seeds

Steps:

1. Add the butter, brown sugar, and molasses to a medium-sized bowl. Use an electric mixer and beat everything together until the butter is creamy.

2. In another bowl, mix the flour, masa harina, baking powder, and salt together. Pour half into the butter mixture. Mix until combined. Then, add the rest of the dry ingredients and mix again. Stir in the vanilla.

3. Cover and refrigerate the dough for 15 minutes. Preheat oven to 350 degrees.

4. Divide the dough in half. On a clean, lightly floured surface, roll a dough half to about ⅛-inch thickness. Use a round cookie cutter or a clean drinking glass to cut cookies about 3 inches in diameter. You can also roll smaller dough balls and use the bottom of a glass or a heavy pan to press cookie shapes instead.

5. Set the cookies on a greased baking sheet, about 2 inches apart. Keep making cookies until all the dough is used. Sprinkle each cookie with sesame seeds.

6. Bake cookies until golden brown. Check after 10 minutes, and then continue checking every couple of minutes until they are done.

7. Cool the cookies completely before enjoying.

Tip: If you have a sesame seed allergy, you can make these cookies without them. Sprinkle the cookies with sugar instead to keep some of the crunch.

What a fun day! I learned so much—I feel like I tasted food straight out of Mexican and Central American kitchens. Now I have recipe cards to take home. My family is going to love helping me make these dishes.

The culture and food of Central America are so rich. Corn and beans are important crops. They show up in many recipes. But each country has its own way of making those flavors unique. Even if people leave their homelands, they take their food along with them. Never be afraid to try new things. Food helps us learn about other places in the world without ever going there.

Eating authentic food is the fastest way to learn about people and places. Sharing those flavors with others spreads that joy even further.

Trying something new can be fun. Food is meant to be enjoyed and celebrated!

Recipe: Taste the World!
(Made with love by the chefs in this kitchen.)

Mari Bolte is a Korean adoptee who loves cooking and trying out new recipes! Her favorite places are Asian markets and specialty grocery stores.

Mom and designer Alyx Douglas creates whimsical stories with the goal of introducing children to different cultures and their cuisines. She lives in Philadelphia where she enjoys going to locally owned restaurants featuring diverse and authentic flavors with her family.

Amber Gayle is a Southeast Asian illustrator in Ohio with a passion for bringing colorful and expressive characters to life. She is a children's book illustrator and background artist.

Manuel Román-Lacayo is a Nicaraguan American cultural heritage expert who has visited nearly every country in the Americas as a researcher and consultant. Having lived in Costa Rica, Nicaragua, and Guatemala, he loves tortillas, gallo pinto, and champurradas. He lives in Pittsburgh with his wife, two sons, and a bunch of bicycles.